boy shirt— buttons on <u>this</u> side ↓

girl shirt — buttons on <u>that</u> side (don't ask me why!) ↑ ↑

father shoe ↓

W9-AZB-091

↑ what are the little holes for? Feet air-conditioning?

father color— plaid ↑

Amelia's Family Ties

OR KNOTS? →

shaving cream or clown makeup ↓

knotty knot ↑

by Marissa Moss

(and dutiful daughter? Amelia)

scrapbook for cozy family memories ↑

American Girl

father slipper— no fuzz, <u>not</u> pink ↑

If you're a man, it's called after-shave lotion. If you're a woman, it's called toilet water. (Yucch!) Whatever you call it, it stinks!

father toilet— put the seat down! ↑

SCHOLASTIC INC.

New York Toronto London Auckland Sydney
Mexico City New Delhi Hong Kong Buenos Aires

moosaic cow

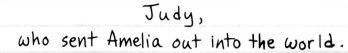

moovie star cow

This notebook is dedicated to
Judy,
who sent Amelia out into the world.

ISBN 0-439-39063-X

moosical
cow

12 11 10 9 8 7 6 5 4 3   2 3 4 5 6 7/0

elevator going down!

elevator going up!

Printed in the U.S.A.   24

First Scholastic printing, February 2002

Book design by Amelia

mootant
cow →

It looked like an ordinary letter. ↘

1863 Chickamauga #12C
Chicago, IL 60611

APRICOTS 74

flowers
26¢

TICK
TICK

Amelia
564 N. Homerest
Oopa, OR 97881

I'll be 90 years old before I spell this stupid word right!

It felt like a time bomb! ↗

I love getting mail, even junk mail, but when I saw this letter I was almost afraid to open it. I could tell from the return address that it was from my dad. My dad — it's ~~wierd~~ ~~weird~~ ~~wierd~~ weird to even say that.

I don't remember him at all. Cleo doesn't either, so she's no help, and Mom won't talk about him. At least she finally gave me his address so I could write to him. But that was months and months ago. I'd given up hope that he would write back, but he did!

Mom handed me the letter, but she didn't look happy about it. After all this time, she's still mad at him.

What if the letter told me to BUG OFF!?

What if he said he hated me and that's why he left in the first place? After all, right after I was born, he was gone.

Cleo was really curious— she kept trying to stick her jelly roll nose in my letter.

Can I read it, too? C'mon, he's _my_ dad, too.

No way! It's to _me_. Write your _own_ letter to him if you want a letter back.

This is the ONLY thing I've _ever_ gotten from my dad.

Dear Amelia,

I've written this letter a dozen times trying to think of the right thing to say, but I'm afraid there's no good excuse for not writing to you earlier. I meant to get a divorce from your mother, not from you and your sister. But I'm a journalist, and I began working in Japan after the divorce. I was there for ten years. From that distance, it seemed too difficult to stay in contact with a toddler (Cleo) and a baby (you).

Now I'm back in the United States, in Chicago. I've remarried and have a new family. You're a big sister now. Your baby brother George is six months old.

You have every reason to be angry with me, but now that you've found me, I'd like to stay found. I'd like to be part of your life. If you want to be part of mine, too, I hope you'll come spend a week with me this summer. You'll get to know me, my wife, Clara, and your half-brother. I've already talked to your mother, and she's agreed you can come. Think about it. I hope you decide to find out who your father really is.

Dad

What if I went and he didn't like me?

What if he disappeared __again__ after meeting me?

Did I want to meet him? Of course I did! But I noticed he didn't sign the letter "Love, Dad," just "Dad." And being in Japan was a pretty lame excuse for not writing all this time. I __know__ they have mail there because my pen pal, Mako, lives in Japan, and he writes me __all__ the time.

I don't even know what it feels like to have a dad.

← possible dads →

Did you hear the one about the banana? Ha ha!

laughs-too-loud, jokey dad

Not now, honey, I'm busy.

working-all-the-time, business-guy dad

We had to walk 20 miles to school — in the snow!

lecturing, when-I-was-your-age dad

roll of the dad dice — which kind of dad will I get?

Mom was waiting for me to finish reading the letter. "Well," she asked, "do you want to go?"

I wanted to say yes and I wanted to say no, so I didn't say anything.

"Go where?" asked Cleo, the nosy one.

"Your father has invited both of you to visit sometime this summer," Mom said. "One at a time, so he can get to know you."

Other kids go to summer camp — I go to a new family.
At least I won't get a lot of bug bites.

Don't forget to pack your marshmallows!

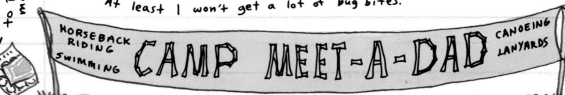

HORSEBACK RIDING SWIMMING CAMP MEET-A-DAD CANOEING LANYARDS

Cleo couldn't <u>wait</u> to go, but he invited me first. I hated the idea that she might meet him before I did.

I'm the oldest — I'll go first!

A Cleo-type dad would look like this.

"I'll go," I said. "But I'm not going to like him. I'm just curious to see if he's anything like Cleo."

So it's settled. I'm going to fly on an airplane all by myself to a strange city (Chicago) to meet a strange man (my dad). The whole thing sounds **STRANGE!**

Cleo's jealous that I'm going to meet our dad first, so she's being extra mean.

If he <u>is</u> like Cleo, it will be TERRIBLE! He'll snore, chew with his mouth WIDE open, and get carsick—yucch!

You'll ruin my chance!

I should go first! If you go, he'll never want to see another kid as long as he lives!

TRA LA LA LA! I can't <u>hear</u> you! TRA LA LA!

I had to write my friend Nadia about it.

Dear Nadia,
    Guess what? My dad finally wrote me back! I'm going to visit him in a couple of weeks. Do you have any advice about how to act around a dad? Are dads the same as moms? Mom says she's <u>nothing</u> like Dad, and that's one reason they're divorced. What if he's like a grown-up Cleo? **SCARY!**

luv, amelia
yours till the cake walks!

WAKE UP AND 20¢
SMELL THE COFFEE

Nadia Kurz
61 South St.
Barton, CA 91010

Hi!

I'm chocolate!

When she got my card, Nadia called, and after we talked, I felt much better.

C'mon, Amelia, I bet you've got a cool dad.

If he were really cool, he wouldn't have left.

Just give him a chance. And have fun — you'll be in a cool new city.

I'll try.

Carly's been great, too. But then, she has her _own_ reasons for wanting me to meet my dad.

Carly has a whole list of questions for me to ask my dad. She's excited that he's a reporter, because that's what she wants to be.

Ask him where he went to school, how he got his first job, which newspaper he thinks is the best to work for, what's the difference between writing for magazines and newspapers, where he's trav...

But the question I want to ask is why? Why did he leave, and why did he stay away, and why doesn't he care about us?

At the airport, Cleo gave me a package to give our dad. She said if I dared to open it, she'd tear me apart. She looked like she meant it, too.

Cleo's gift for Dad — I don't even want to open it.

It's probably a stupid joke T-shirt like the one she gave Mom for Mother's Day.

BECAUSE I SAID SO!

Cleo's idea of a good Mom present

I gave Mom a hug, and then the flight attendant led me on the plane like I was a baby. I was excited about getting to fly all by myself, but a nosy lady sat next to me and she wouldn't stop talking. She wanted to know where I was going, who was going to meet me, if I was excited, and yakkity shmakkity. I told her I was an orphan going to meet a family that might want to adopt me, but three families had rejected me already, so I didn't expect them to like me. She looked at me like I was a hardened criminal and didn't say another word.

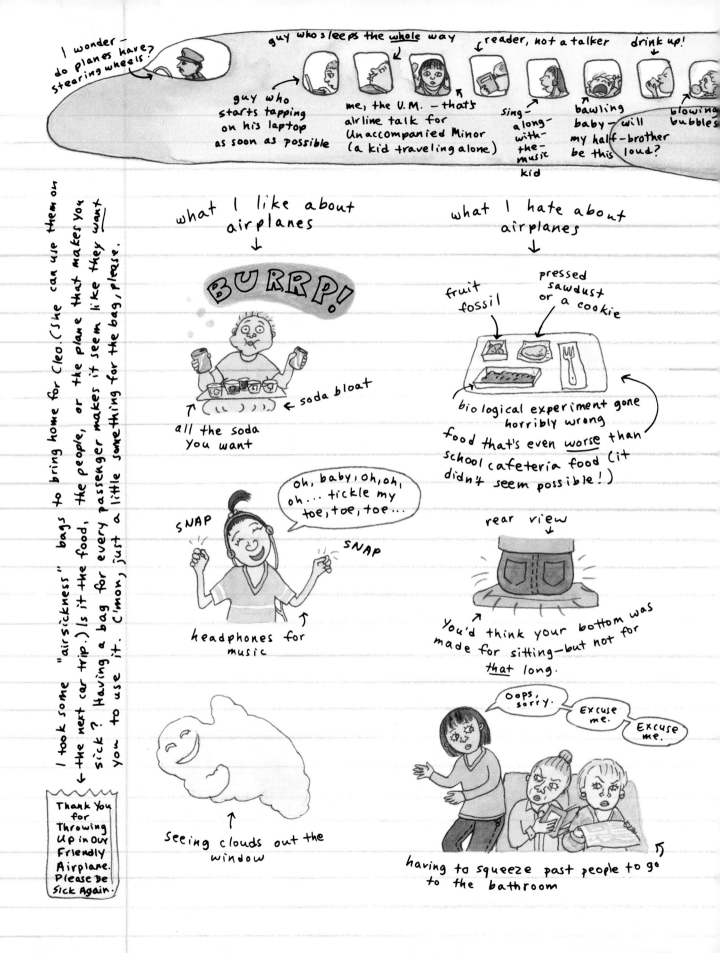

putting on lipstick

brushing teeth— some people think the plane is a private bathroom

nightie-night!

peanut guzzler

way too much soda!

privacy, please

the real hazard of air travel— getting stuck and squashed behind a snoring machine! There go my knees!

ZZZZZZZ

Help! I'm trapped!

Fortunately, just when I thought I'd go crazy being smushed on that plane, the pilot announced we'd be on the ground in 10 minutes. HOORAY!

When the plane started to land, I started to get nervous. What if this whole thing was a big mistake? What if I went home with the wrong person? Mom said Dad would have to sign for me like I was some kind of special delivery. Surprise, here's the package — me!

Before I could run and hide in the bathroom, the flight attendant gave me some plastic wings and led me off the plane to a man who was waiting there.

souvenir of my U.M. flight →

← cheapo, stick-on wings

I knew right away who he was — he had Cleo's nose!

He was kind of smiling, kind of not, like he was the one who was nervous.

He didn't look anything like me — so maybe he was just Cleo's dad, not mine.

He was carrying a teddy bear for me, like I was a baby or something.

I had tried to imagine his voice and face so many times. Now here he was — and he wasn't at all like I'd imagined. (Except he did have a head, two hands, and two feet.)

When he saw how big I was, he said he was sorry, but he didn't know what ten-year-olds were like. I said I didn't know what ten-year-olds were like either — I only knew what I was like.

I haven't seen anyone wear penny loafers since Mr. Nudel, my fourth-grade teacher. I hoped it was a good sign — I like Mr. Nudel a lot. Maybe my dad will be at least a little bit like my old teacher.

So, Amelia, at last we meet! I know this is strange.

We'll both just have to get used to each other. Want to shake on it?

He did most of the talking. I couldn't think of what to say.

I didn't want to shake his hand, but I did. I noticed he had hair on his knuckles — GROSS! But I was polite and didn't say anything about it.

Dad kept asking questions — about Cleo and Mom, where we lived and where we went to school. I felt like yelling, "You'd know this stuff already if you cared about us!" He kept on talking like he was afraid of it being quiet. He talked about Chicago and pointed out famous places when we drove past them. He talked about his wife, Clara, who's a veterinarian, and about baby George and how smart and cute he was. (I felt very un-smart and un-cute.)

Chicago is a BIG city with lots of TALL buildings, but we drove into a neighborhood with beautiful old houses. (You could still see the skyscrapers.)

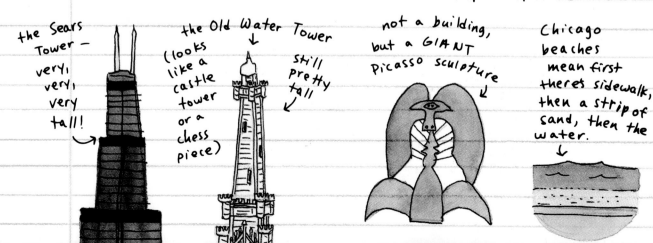

the Sears Tower — very, very, very tall!

the Old Water Tower (looks like a castle tower or a chess piece)

still pretty tall

not a building, but a GIANT Picasso sculpture

Chicago beaches mean first there's sidewalk, then a strip of sand, then the water.

cup of cow-fee

Of all the things my dad pointed out, my favorite was the cows. They weren't real, but sculptures, all painted and decorated differently, all over the city. They're part of a special outdoor art exhibit called "Chi-Cow-Go." (Chi-cow-go - Chicago - very funny!)

midnight cowboy

I thought it would be so cool to live in one of those old houses, but Dad parked in the garage of the ugliest concrete box I'd ever seen.

cowsmonaut

100% cowton

cowabunga

nice, cozy old house
(It took forever to draw this, but it was the closest I could come to getting such a nice home.)

booooring modern apartment building
(at least it has a view of the pretty house

I got out of the car. I still didn't feel like his daughter. And he didn't feel like a dad to me, excep I didn't know what that would feel like.

cowsonants

cowtinents

cownfusion

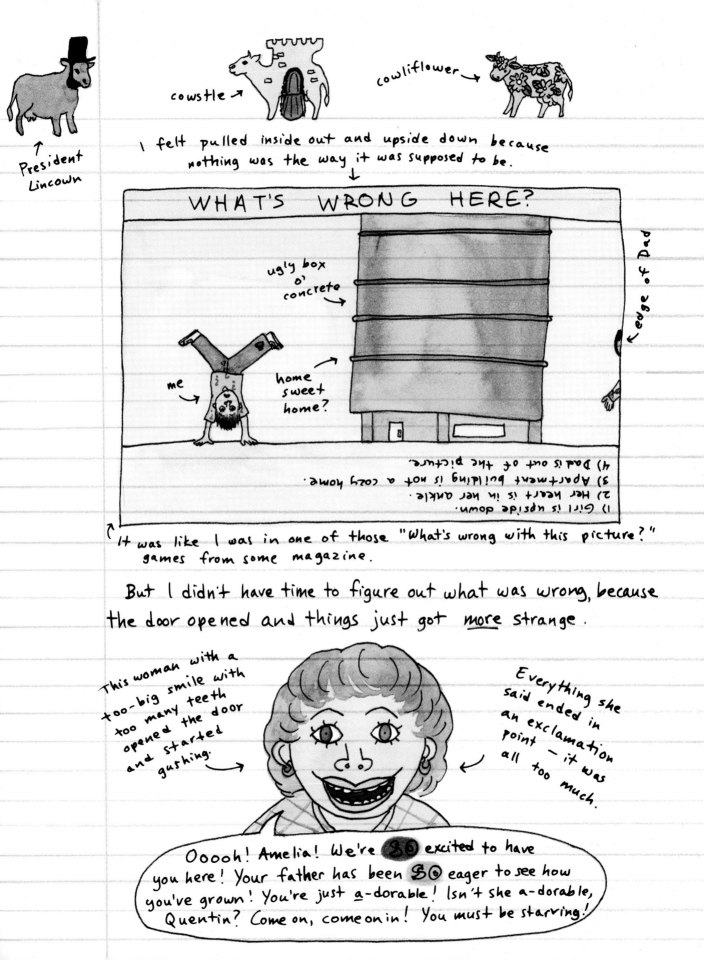

What-in-cownation!

← excowmation points

step-cow

shopping cowt

That was Clara. Technically, she's my stepmother, but I definitely wouldn't call her Mom. I just stood there, so Dad nudged me into the apartment.

"Welcome home, Amelia," he said. (At least he didn't talk in exclamation points.) "Let's go meet your brother." Half-brother, I said to myself, but I followed Dad into a room crammed with teddy bears. (Dad added my bear to the pile, I noticed.)

George was asleep in his crib, and I had to admit, he was very cute. Thank goodness he doesn't have a jelly roll nose.

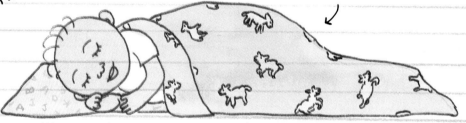

It's o.k. George, you can have my bear.

I couldn't help it, I fell in love with George right away. I stroked his soft cheek gently with my finger.

"Hey, little brother," I whispered. "It's me, Amelia, your sister." He opened his eyes, looked right at me, and smiled. He grabbed my finger, and for the first time today, something felt right.

George's hand is so tiny, my finger looked like a giant's next to his. →

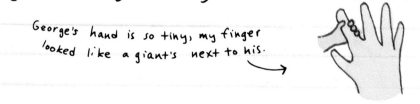

Clara said I could hold George after she changed his diaper, so while I was waiting, I gave Dad the present from Cleo. (See, Cleo, I didn't open it, not even for a peek!)

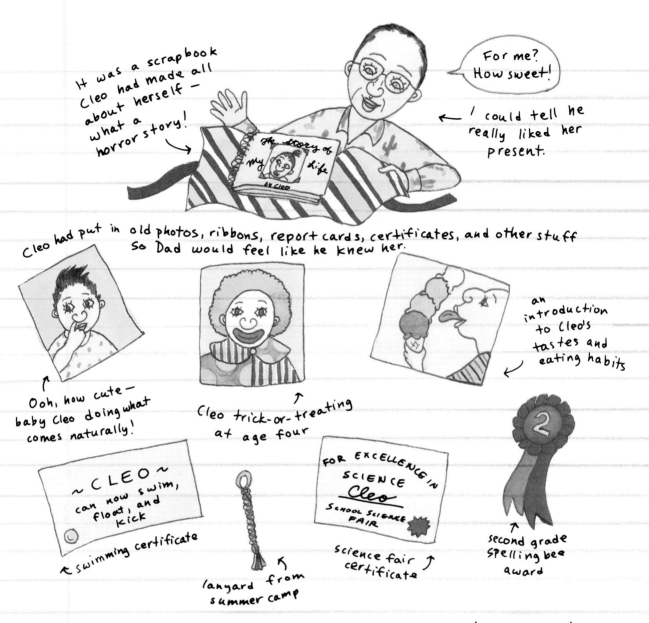

It was a scrapbook Cleo had made all about herself — what a horror story!

The story of my life
by Cleo

For me? How sweet!

I could tell he really liked her present.

Cleo had put in old photos, ribbons, report cards, certificates, and other stuff so Dad would feel like he knew her.

an introduction to Cleo's tastes and eating habits

Ooh, how cute — baby Cleo doing what comes naturally!

Cleo trick-or-treating at age four

~ CLEO ~ can now swim, float, and kick

swimming certificate

lanyard from summer camp

FOR EXCELLENCE IN SCIENCE
Cleo
SCHOOL SCIENCE FAIR

science fair certificate

2

second grade spelling bee award

Dad smiled and said I have an amazing sister. Great! He already likes Cleo better than me. Well, I don't care, because I don't like him.

I said I was tired and went to my room. I felt like crying. What had I expected, anyway? What did I want?

I'm sleeping in the guest room. It's Dad's office when he works at home, but there's a fold-out couch, too. ↘

view of nice houses

Japanese prints

telephone — I wish I could call Nadia

computer — at least I can e-mail Nadia and Carly if I'm desperate

sofa bed

file cabinets

It was a nice room, better than I thought from the outside, but I couldn't get comfortable.

I guess I wanted "Instant Happy Family."

Just add one dad (o.k., a stepmother and half-brother, too), mix well together, and bake.

Yum! Smells delicious!

You'll love it — satisfaction guaranteed or we'll send you a new "Instant Happy Family."

When prepared as instructed, you get this. ↘

Beware! If you're careless, you'll end up with an unsightly mess. ↘

I dreamed I baked up a new family, only instead of people, I got a cake. When I woke up, I was still here, with Dad, Clara, and George, but I did smell cake — pancakes! That was a good way to start the day.

After breakfast, we went to the zoo. I thought it would be fun, but it seemed as if I was behind bars being watched all the time, the most strange animal of them all. Dad and Clara looked at me as though I were about to explode — and they asked the stupidest questions ever.

I tried to imagine we were a normal family, like all the other families at the zoo. But I didn't feel normal. And I didn't feel like this was my family.

So, do you like your school, Amelia? How's your house?

Do you play soccer?

Gabool!

Did you have a good teacher?

What's your favorite subject in school?

My question is, "Why do grown-ups ask so many questions?" What if I asked them, "Do you like your work? Do you have a good boss? Do you play soccer? What's your favorite breakfast cereal?" What I really wanted to ask was, "Why did you leave, Dad?" and "Is it true you picked the name Amelia? Why? Do I mean anything to you?" But I'm too scared to ask those questions.

rub-a-dub-dub
a George in
a tub →

The best part of the day was giving George his bath. He laughed when I played games with him, and he has the most beautiful smile. I didn't know it would be so much fun to be a big sister. Cleo always complains about it. But then she's not very good at it. I can tell that George thinks I'm a perfect sister.

BABY PAGE

The care and feeding of a baby:

WAA!

It's harder than it looks to get a shirt over a baby's head!

More food will end up on the floor, the ceiling, and the outside of the baby than _inside_ the baby. Careful! Don't step in the pea puddle.

Magaaa!

I asked George if he knew why Dad left Mom, but he just said "Maga." <u>That's</u> no answer.

George already feels like family, but is he? Funny how a baby fits into my family right away. I guess grown-ups take longer. (Well, they're not as cute, that's for sure!)

Gaa!

Baby's hands may be tiny, but they can pull hair <u>hard</u>!

I felt as if I could tell George ANYTHING. The only problem is, he can't say anything back. Unless you count "Bagoosh."

The person I really needed to talk to was Nadia, so I decided to e-mail her.

<u>Always</u> put a towel on your shoulder when you burp a baby!

To: Nadia
From: Amelia
Subject: Family

Nadia,
  Help! Get me outta here! :C The only person I like is my baby brother. He's very cute. But still, he can't TALK to me.
                    Amelia

Do <u>not</u> jiggle the baby after he eats — you'll be sorry!

EXTREMELY IMPORTANT!!! WARNING!!
Always cover the baby with a diaper when you change him.

squirt preventer

If you don't, you'll get squirted — right in the face!

Clara collects these miniature shoes— what's that about? Mom would NEVER have these!

Zebra shoe

Cinderella slipper

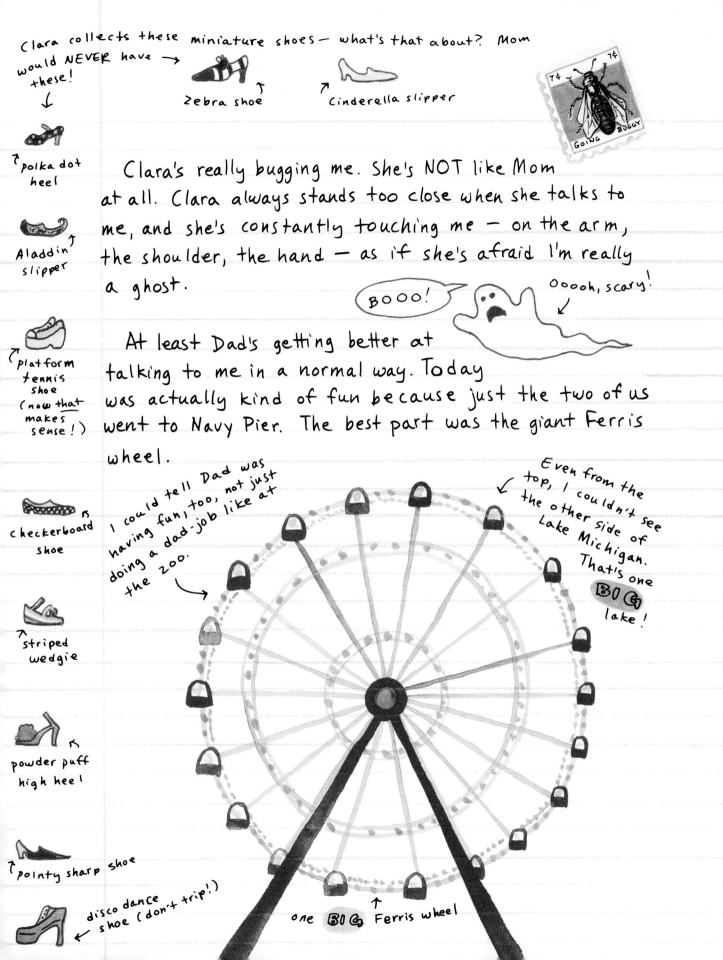

polka dot heel

Aladdin slipper

platform tennis shoe (now that makes sense!)

checkerboard shoe

striped wedgie

powder puff high heel

pointy sharp shoe

disco dance shoe (don't trip!)

Clara's really bugging me. She's NOT like Mom at all. Clara always stands too close when she talks to me, and she's constantly touching me — on the arm, the shoulder, the hand — as if she's afraid I'm really a ghost.

BOOO!

Ooooh, scary!

At least Dad's getting better at talking to me in a normal way. Today was actually kind of fun because just the two of us went to Navy Pier. The best part was the giant Ferris wheel.

I could tell Dad was having fun, too, not just doing a dad-job like at the zoo.

Even from the top, I couldn't see the other side of Lake Michigan. That's one BIG lake!

one BIG Ferris wheel

This candy looks good, but → tastes terrible.

↑ watermelon ribbon

licorice sandwich

syrup a wa bo

Then we went to a GREAT candy store, and I got to pick out a ton of candy. Grown-ups only let you do stuff like that when they feel guilty. That's fine with me — I can eat the candy without feeling sweet about the person who bought it.

gummy ↗ penguin

The BEST part of all was when I got back to the apartment. I checked my e-mail and there was a message from Nadia! Now I don't feel so alone.

↗ To eat or not to eat, that is the questio

Too sweet not too su that is t questi

↑ gummy gums (and teeth!)

To: Amelia
From: Nadia
Subject: Family Ties

Amelia,
Give your dad and stepmom a chance. After all, you only just met them. It takes a while to get to know someone. Remember how shy I was with you at first? I bet things will get better (and if they don't, think of it as a vacation from Cleo). :)

Nadia

Maybe Nadia's right. Every day things get a little easier. Maybe we're all getting used to each other. Even Clara wasn't as annoying tonight.

← candy to build with →

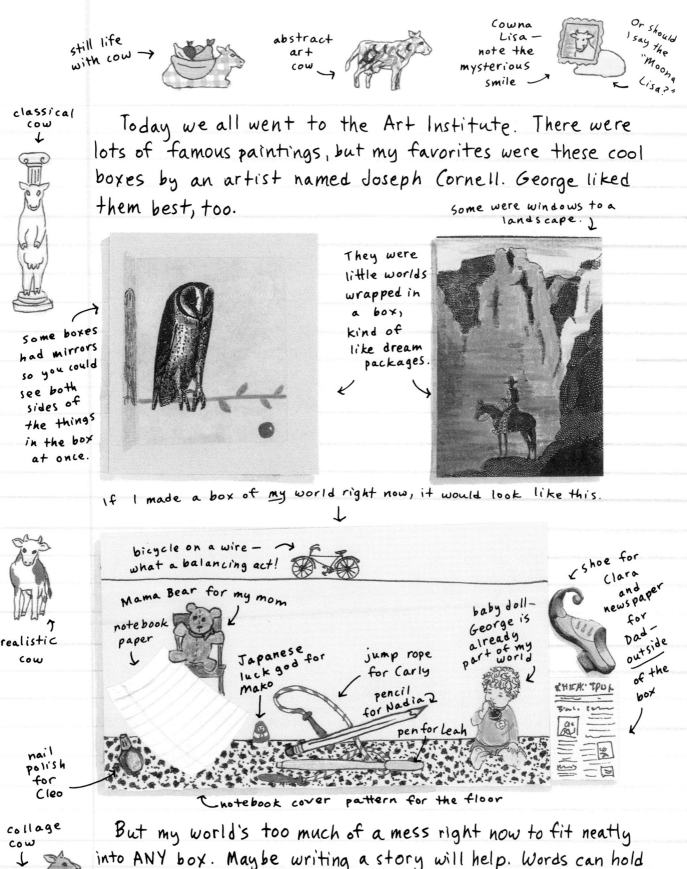

still life with cow →

abstract art cow →

Cowna Lisa — note the mysterious smile →

Or should I say the "Moona Lisa?" ←

classical cow ↓

Today we all went to the Art Institute. There were lots of famous paintings, but my favorites were these cool boxes by an artist named Joseph Cornell. George liked them best, too.

Some were windows to a landscape. ↓

They were little worlds wrapped in a box, kind of like dream packages.

Some boxes had mirrors so you could see both sides of the things in the box at once.

If I made a box of _my_ world right now, it would look like this. ↓

bicycle on a wire — what a balancing act!

Mama Bear for my mom

notebook paper ↓

realistic cow ↑

Japanese luck god for Mako

jump rope for Carly

pencil for Nadia ↓

pen for Leah

baby doll — George is already part of my world

shoe for Clara and newspaper for Dad — _outside_ of the box ↓

nail polish for Cleo

notebook cover pattern for the floor

collage cow ↓

But my world's too much of a mess right now to fit neatly into ANY box. Maybe writing a story will help. Words can hold a _lot_ of stuff. Anyway, writing always makes me feel better.

I look at George, who is _so_ adorable, and I think I must have been that cute when I was a baby. Why didn't my dad adore _me_?

a story  starting here

The Orphan

Once there was a boy who didn't have any parents. And he was happy that way. He lived by himself in a little house, and he could eat pizza for breakfast and not make his bed, and no one would nag him about it.

But one day a man and a woman came to his house. "Oh, you poor thing," they said. "You must be so sad and lonely. How would you like it if _we_ lived with you and took care of you, and you could call us Mom and Dad?"

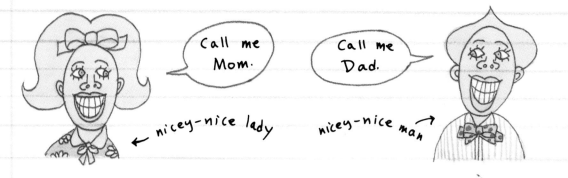

Call me Mom.

Call me Dad.

← nicey-nice lady

nicey-nice man →

The boy _didn't_ like it, but he didn't know what to say. The man and the woman didn't wait for an answer anyway. They barged right in and started acting like parents.

"Go clean your room," said the dad.

"And then we'll have some nice brussels sprouts and liver for dinner," said the mom.

a deadly combination! →

→ two horrible smells, two terrible tastes in one awful meal!

Things to pack

markers

cozy, warm pajamas

comic books

favorite shirt

fuzzy bunny slippers

science stuff

notebooks

Things to leave behind

toothbrush and toothpaste

suspicious green vegetables

napkins

The boy went to his room, but he didn't clean it. There was only one thing to do. He packed a suitcase with all his favorite stuff, climbed out the window, and ran away.

He found a new little house, even nicer than the first one, and he lived happily ever after.

cold, thick Chicago-style pizza for breakfast

Yum!

hair not combed

unmade bed — how cozy!

never-ending game of Monopoly left on the floor — why bother to clean it up?

The End

It happened! Worse than a mountain of brussels sprouts! Worse than making a million beds! Just when I thought MAYBE things were getting better, things got WAY, WAY WORSE!

RED ALERT!

I've been mad at my mom. I've been mad at Leah. I've been mad at Cleo. But I've <u>never</u> been as mad at anyone as I am at Clara.

SHE READ MY NOTEBOOK!

I couldn't believe it! At dinner, she turned to me and said, "So, you're a writer, like your dad. You're really good."
I asked her what she meant. And she said, "Well, I saw that story in your notebook—"

ENEMY INVASION! CONTAMINATION HAS OCCURRED!

I EXPLODED!

All the stuff I'd kept inside came pouring out.
"HOW COULD YOU?! THAT'S PRIVATE!!
HOW WOULD YOU LIKE IT IF I READ YOUR
DIARY OR YOUR LETTERS?!

I HATE YOU!"

I ran into my room and SLAMMED the door.
I was so ANGRY I didn't know what to do, but I knew
I couldn't stay in that apartment one minute longer.
I started packing my suitcase. Maybe I could get an earlier
flight home. If I couldn't, I'd just live at the airport until
it was time to go.

all the comforts of home

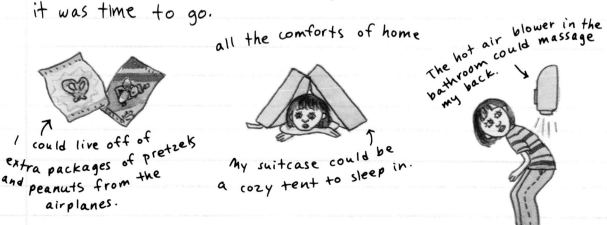

I could live off of extra packages of pretzels and peanuts from the airplanes.

My suitcase could be a cozy tent to sleep in.

The hot air blower in the bathroom could massage my back.

First thing I did was to decontaminate my notebook.

It took 17 tissues to wipe every page.

When I finished packing, I just huddled on the sofa, looking out the window. Why was everything turning out so bad? From this ugly concrete building to this ugly concrete lump in my stomach.

Are better lives happening just across the street? Do the people in pretty houses lead prettier lives?

I just _had_ to talk to someone, so I called Nadia. I told her what had happened and that I was packed and ready to go.

"But Amelia," Nadia said, "you don't have to like Clara, just put up with her. How are things with your dad? That's the main question."

I told her the main question wasn't answered yet. Maybe it never would be. When Nadia heard that, she said I should definitely stick it out. "You've got to get to know your father better, and he has to learn who _you_ are." She's right. Nadia usually is.

Even though I couldn't see Nadia, her voice made me feel she was right there with me.

I thought Dad would see my suitcase ready to go and be so glad to get rid of me, he'd drive me → to the airport right away.

Dad knocked quietly on the door and came in. I thought he'd yell at me for yelling at Clara, but he didn't. He looked very sad.

"I'm sorry, Amelia," he said. (It seems like he's always apologizing to me.) "What Clara did was wrong. I'm shocked she read your notebook, but I promise you — she promises you — it won't happen again. She didn't understand how important your notebook is to you, but I do." He smiled a little. "Because I kept one, too, when I was your age."

That was a surprise. Part of me was still mad, but part of me wondered what kind of notebook he had and did he still have it? Did he like to draw the way I do? Would I ever get to see his notebook? Are boys' notebooks different from girls'?

sports notebook →

comic notebook ↙

regular notebook ↗

science notebook ↓

It's funny, but knowing about his notebook made me feel like he really is my father. Cleo may have his nose, but I have his writing.

"You're packed," Dad said, looking at my suitcase.
I still didn't say anything.
Dad kneeled in front of me and took my hands. They may have been hairy, but his hands felt warm and strong. I didn't want him to let go.

My little hand in his big one was like George's tiny fingers in mine. →

"Listen, Amelia," he said, "I know I've been a terrible father, and I keep saying and doing the wrong things, but I AM trying. Please stay."

He even had tears in his eyes! I didn't know dads could cry. I wanted to hug him, but I couldn't. All I could do was nod my head.

For a minute I thought _he_ was going to hug _me_. But he didn't. He patted my head softly instead.

"Thank you," he said, and he left.

After he was gone, the room felt thick and cottony with quiet. I was more alone than ever.

I didn't want to cry, but I could feel the tears in my eyes. Maybe what he said should have been enough, but it wasn't. I lay in bed and cried until I fell asleep.

what do I want from him, anyway? What do I expect?

My heart feels all broken to pieces, but I can't say why.

Usually writing things down helps me figure them out, but not today.

I can't draw what's wrong, either — I don't know _what_ to draw.

It all looks normal, but <u>nothing's</u> the same anymore. →

Simple spoon →

regular old bowl ↑

ordinary box of cereal ←

It was hard to get up and act like everything was normal this morning. Clara said how sorry she was, but then she acted like she didn't want to be around me. She rushed off to work, leaving Dad, George, and me alone, which was fine by me.

DANGER! bomb about to EXPLODE! ↑ Amelia

George was the only one who acted the way he always does, smearing cereal up his nose and in his ears. ↓

Dad tried to be all jokey as he ate oatmeal, pretending to be Papa Bear. →

It looks like cereal, but acts like face cream. ↑

Then Dad had to go to work in his office — that is, in my bedroom. He said he had an important phone interview and asked me to watch George. I'd never taken care of a baby all by myself, but I didn't think it'd be hard.

handful of mush →

My first job was to wash off all the dried-on cereal — yucch! ←

what's the point of the bib? Oatmeal still goes EVERYWHERE! →

food or toy? ←

And at first, it wasn't. I read George a book, and we played with his toys. Then suddenly he erupted, like a science-fair volcano!

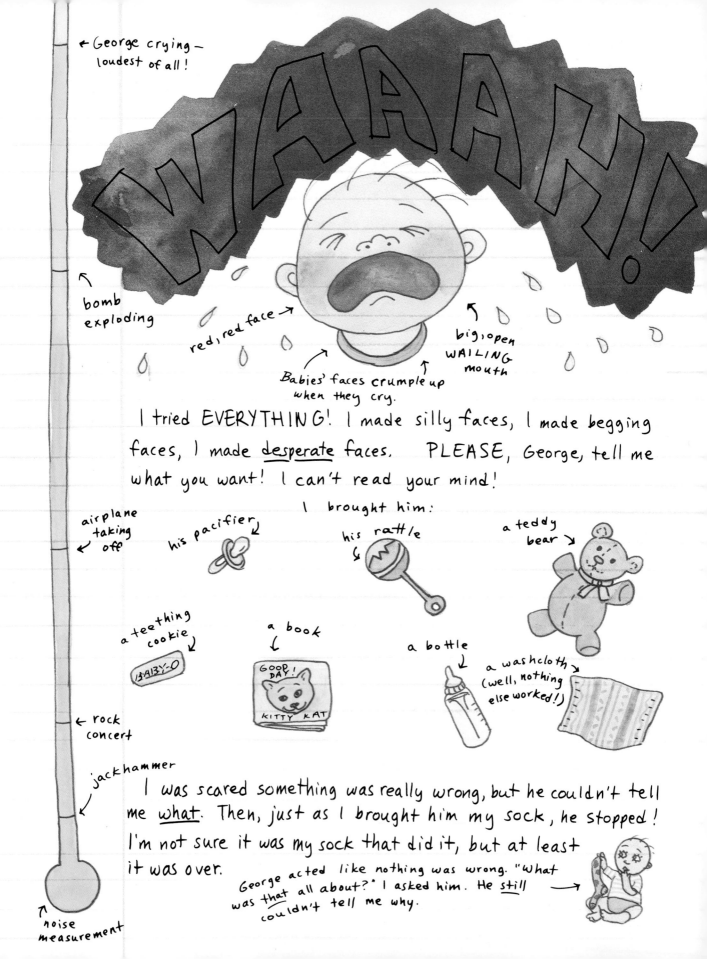

← George crying — loudest of all!

WAAAH!!

bomb exploding

red, red face →

big, open WAILING mouth

Babies' faces crumple up when they cry.

I tried EVERYTHING! I made silly faces, I made begging faces, I made <u>desperate</u> faces. PLEASE, George, tell me what you want! I can't read your mind!

airplane taking off

I brought him:

his pacifier

his rattle

a teddy bear

a teething cookie
BABY-O

a book
GOOD DAY!
KITTY KAT

a bottle

a washcloth (well, nothing else worked!)

← rock concert

jackhammer

I was scared something was really wrong, but he couldn't tell me <u>what</u>. Then, just as I brought him my sock, he stopped! I'm not sure it was my sock that did it, but at least it was over.

George acted like nothing was wrong. "What was <u>that</u> all about?" I asked him. He <u>still</u> couldn't tell me why. →

↑ noise measurement

rock from
Antarctica

block from
Westminster
← Abbey

← brick from
Abraham
Lincoln's
home

Tribune
Tower ↓

After Clara got home, Dad took me to see his real office at the newspaper. The inside was a regular work-type place — desks, computers, phones — but the outside was amazing! The building is old, so it's pretty (not just a block of concrete), but the best part was all these different rocks and parts of buildings taken from all over the world and stuck into the outside walls, kind of how we stuck treasures in the wet concrete at my school.

part of the
Great Pyramid
in Giza,
Egypt ↓

block from
the Roman
Colosseum

But the best rock of all was inside of the building — a moon rock! →

This was really out of this world!

The Apollo 15 astronauts brought it back with them.

Stone George
Washington
landed on
when he crossed
the Delaware

Seeing all these different bits and pieces made me want to go on a trip around the world. I bet Dad's been to a lot of these places. Maybe next time, he'll take me. (If I want to go with him, that is.)

This was a slooow drawing! ↗

head from the
House of Parliament
in London

decoration
from the Mosque of
Suleiman the Magnificent
in Istanbul

stone from
King David's
tower in
Jerusalem ↓

ornament
from the
bridge in the
Forbidden City
in
Beijing ↓

rock from "Injun Joe's" cave, Missouri (from Mark Twain's book)

stone from the Alamo in Texas

chip off the Berlin wall in Germany (when there was a Berlin wall)

from the Arch of Triumph in Paris

This is my daughter, Amelia

Dad introduced me to everyone as his daughter and he didn't even seem embarrassed. →

It looked hard to write for a newspaper. You have to write fast, and you can't make up whatever you want to happen (like in my stories). I don't think I'll be that kind of writer when I grow up.

We went to a place called the morgue, only it wasn't full of dead people, just more computers, photo files, and old newspapers. Dad wanted to show me some articles he'd written. I have to admit, it was cool seeing his name in print like that. (But what I'd really like to read is one of his notebooks — with his permission, of course. I'm not a snoop like Clara!)

He gave me an article to keep from his "clip file" (no, not toenail clippings — newspaper clippings!).
↓

In Japan, Work Is Play

The politeness and civility of the Japanese is legendary. What's not so widely understood is how this affects the sense of community and common changes rub against the grain, but no more so than in older, more conservative sectors of populations in general. We, as

stone from Independence Hall in Pennsylvania

decoration from the Cathedral of Notre Dame in Paris

rock from the Parthenon in Athens →

ornament from the Santa Sophia in Istanbul →

I tried to remember all the questions Carly wanted me to ask about being a reporter, but I couldn't. Dad said he'd call Carly and talk to her himself. I'm glad somebody's getting something out of this visit.

Dad's desk

In Japan he was a foreign correspondent, so he wrote about stuff that happened there. Now he writes for the editorial page.

stone from the Great Wall of China

Seeing his office made me feel funny — like I was part of his life, but I wasn't. There were photos of Clara and George, but not of me and Cleo. Would he put some up now, add us to his family collection? He still didn't feel like my dad. I was getting bits and pieces of him, like the stones on the building, but it wasn't enough.

rock from Bunker Hill, Massachusetts

Back at the apartment, I could tell Clara still didn't want to be around me. Dad could tell, too, because he put on a fake happy voice and said he'd been planning a special night for me — dinner out, just the two of us. I didn't care about dinner, but maybe he'd finally tell me what I wanted to know.

tile from Forbidden City in Beijing

← cow from Roy's Steak House in Fresno (just kidding — I wanted to get a cow in)

stone from → St. Peter's Cathedral in Rome

stone from Tower of Tears in Amsterdam ↗

The Dinner

glow of candlelight →

Fancy restaurants do not have:

↑ toothpicks with frills on top

packets for mustard and ketchup

↑ non-dairy creamer

french fries — instead they have French Fried Potatoes

The menu was like a heavy book, not the kind printed on a place mat that you're supposed to color on. ↓

Le Menu

The dinner was at a fancy-shmancy restaurant, the kind with cloth napkins and big thick menus with tassels on the ends. I know Dad was trying to be elegant and special, but a diner with a jukebox would have been more my style. There were so many forks, I wasn't sure which one to use. I was afraid I'd make some big embarrassing mistake.

usual kid menu with a maze, word search, and dot-to-dot →

I felt really small. The menu was bigger than my head! →

Pretty nice, huh?

Uh, yeah.

Do they have plain pizza?

At least I got a drink with a little paper umbrella and a maraschino cherry.

I've always wanted one of these. ↓

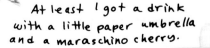

Even the bread was served in a fancy way, with tongs, like something delicate or a jewel. →

More things fancy restaurants don't have:
↓

I ended up with plain spaghetti. (I don't even want to <u>know</u> what foie gras or béchamel are. They sound GROSS — definitely <u>not</u> edible.)

↗ wrapped-up crackers (or <u>any</u> kind of crackers)

Dad talked about living in Japan and the things they eat there (worse than foie gras!) and how he missed it. But what I really wanted to know was why he left us.

Then I remembered how I felt when I was trying to cheer up George. How could I help him if he couldn't tell me what was wrong? And how could Dad know what <u>I</u> needed if I didn't tell him? He couldn't read my mind. So finally I did it. I asked the question.

soda ↗ served in a can

Dad, why did you and Mom get divorced? How come you left us?

Help! My elbow is glued to the table!

↑ sticky table-tops

There was a big silence. I was afraid he hadn't heard me, and I'd never get the nerve to ask again.

But he <u>had</u> heard me. He put his fork down and took a deep breath.

metal napkin holders ↙

plastic utensils — combination spoon and fork →

sugar packets with pictures of Hawaii on them ↗

Things fancy
restaurants
<u>do</u> have:

↓

↑
tablecloths
(and <u>not</u>
checkered
ones)

He looked sad. ↗

Amelia, I'll be honest with you— it was a painful divorce. I needed to travel and couldn't be with your mother as much as she needed. We fought about it for years. It had nothing to do with you or your sister, but after the divorce, your mother and I didn't want to see each other. The two of you were so young, I thought it would be easier if you never knew me.

more forks
than you need
(I don't have
<u>three</u> mouths!)

butter in
little bowls,
not on
squares
of waxed
paper

↓

"Easier for who?" I wanted to know. "For us or for you?"

"I guess for both," Dad said. "But I was wrong. It was a big mistake. I should never have left <u>you</u> just because your mother and I couldn't get along. I'm <u>really</u> sorry."

Even if he <u>was</u> sorry, I still didn't feel better. Something important hadn't been said yet. I wasn't sure what it was, but I'd know it when I heard it.

we both just
sat and stared →
at the napkins
in our laps for
a while. It was my turn to say <u>something</u>. I had to think of what.

"So," I said, "is it true you picked out my name?"

Dad smiled then. "Yes," he said, "I did. When you were born you were so alert already, so eager to be part of the world. I thought you would be a great adventurer, someone willing to take chances, someone like Amelia Earhart."

More things fancy restaurants have: →

↗ Parsley as a decoration on plates (a green vegetable pretty? Are you crazy?!)

Pick me!

No, me!

desserts wheeled to your table on a cart, so you can see what you want to pick, not just read about it

Dad looked right into my eyes and then he said it, what I'd been waiting to hear all this time. "I loved you the minute I saw you."

waitpeople who say, "I'll be your server for tonight" instead of "Whaddya want?"

I couldn't help it, I had to smile. →

I felt like a big weight was gone. ←

↗ a separate menu just for drinks

Suddenly that plain spaghetti tasted like the best spaghetti in the world. We both started eating and talking, and it all felt so perfect. This is what it's like to have a father, I thought. It wasn't hard at all.

Dad even told me baby stories about myself. ↓

Even when I was just a couple of months old, ← I liked to grab onto pens.

And I loved to stare at the ceiling — Dad thought I was turning cracks into pictures. I probably was, too. ↓

Things got better after that. Even Clara! The next morning, she finally looked at me again and really talked to me.

she was being real, not fake-sweet.

she looked like she hadn't slept well in a long time.

I'm new at being a mother — and a stepmother, too. George is teaching me how to be a mom for him, but I don't know how to be a stepmom for a ten-year-old. You'll just have to show me.

will you forgive me?

I looked at George. He was sitting in his high chair grinning at me. I guess since Clara is George's mom, she can't be all bad.

"O.K.," I said, and I started to spoon applesauce into George's mouth.

Best of all, Dad handed me a package.

Not a teddy bear, not candy, not a joke T-shirt, but a ...

... NEW NOTEBOOK! And a whole set of cool Japanese pens!

"I finally found the right present," Dad said. "I just had to find out who you were first."

He opened his arms, and I walked into the first Dad hug of my life.

I'm using my new pens to write a new story.

~ FAMILY LIFE ~

There was this girl who had three different families, all in the same apartment building. On the first floor lived her father and brother, on the second floor lived her mother and sister, on the third floor lived her grandma and grandpa. She ate breakfast with one family, lunch with another, and dinner with another. It was all very confusing.

So the girl had an idea. She sawed holes in the floors and ceilings and put in a long pole like they have in fire stations. Then she could slide from apartment to apartment easily and look up one hole and down another.

Hand me my notebook, please.

Oh no, I left my notebook upstairs! Or was it downstairs?

It was still hard work, going from home to home, but now the girl was happy because she never really had to leave a family behind — there was always a connection.

Sure!

~ THE END ~

Good-bye, cows!

Cowmander cow salutes you!

bro-cow-li cow

cownstruction cow

notebook cow

Tomorrow I'm going home. I'm still figuring out what it means to have a dad. But it's O.K. if I don't have all the answers yet. At least I'm not mad at him anymore, and I know he loves me. Maybe someday I'll even learn to like Clara. For now, I'd say George is my favorite. Even if I'm not sure how to have a father, I'm already an expert on how to have a brother.

me, as a great big sister!

Maybe I have a thing or two to teach Cleo about being an older kid.